UNEXPECTED GUESTS

UNEXPECTED
GUESTS

FAMILY BONDS

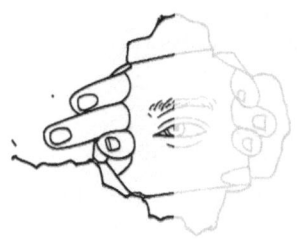

By VANESSA M. GATTIS

UNEXPECTED
GUESTS

Layout design by: *waseem@arrowupz.com*
Edited by: *Antoinette McDonald*
Published by: *Forever And A Day Publishing LLC*
Triangle, VA *www.faadpublishingllc.com*

Paperback ISBN: 979-8-9988364-2-8
eBook ISBN: 979-8-9988364-3-5

First Edition
Printed in the United States of America

For more information about the author, visit:
www.vanessagattis.com

FOREVER AND A DAY PUBLISHING, LLC

DEDICATION

To the unexpected guests in all of our lives—

To the brothers and sisters, sons and daughters, nieces and nephews who walk through our doors carrying more questions than answers, more heart than direction. May this story remind you that love opens doors, grace invites growth, and family—whether born or built—holds the power to change everything.

And to the Aunt Mables and Uncle LeRoys of the world—thank you for keeping the porch light on.

ALSO BY

VANESSA M. GATTIS

CONTENTS

INTRODUCTION

Unexpected Guests: Family Bonds

Big city living isn't for the faint of heart. The hustle, the unpredictability, the pressure to figure life out before you're ready—it's enough to make even the boldest soul question their next step. For young people especially, the city can feel like both a launchpad and a trap. For brothers Doug and Huey, it was a dead end.

Content to coast at home under their mother's roof, the brothers had grown far too comfortable with doing nothing. That comfort came to an abrupt halt the day their mother gave them an ultimatum: get serious about life or get out.

With nowhere else to turn, Doug and Huey boarded a Greyhound bus and headed for Durham, North Carolina—unannounced and uncertain, holding little more than a change of clothes, a bag of groceries, and the hope that family would open the door.

What started as a desperate escape quickly turned into a journey of transformation. In Durham, the boys found not only a place to stay but a place to grow—under the watchful, loving care of Aunt Mable and Uncle LeRoy. They were taught responsibility, respect, and resilience. Along the way, they discovered faith, purpose, and the value of community.

Unexpected Guests: Family Bonds is a heartfelt story of brotherhood, second chances, and the kind of love that meets you where you are—but refuses to let you stay there. Through challenges, laughter, heartaches, and healing, Doug and Huey come to learn that family isn't just who you're born into, it's who shows up when you need them most.

This isn't just a coming-of-age tale. It's a testimony.

Welcome to Durham. The porch light is on.

Chapter One

THE SURPRISE VISIT

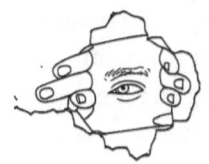

Doug tossed his backpack onto the worn couch and turned to his younger brother; eyes gleaming with excitement.

"Let's go to Durham and visit Aunt Mable for the weekend," he said. "Mom said she retired, and she and Uncle LeRoy have a big house now."

Huey, always the cautious one, frowned. "Shouldn't we call first?"

Doug waved off the concern. "They family. They'll welcome us with open arms."

Huey crossed his arms. "And if they don't?"

"Then we'll cross that bridge when we get there. Mom said we needed to be out of the house before she got back, and we've got a couple hours left. Let's grab something to eat and hit the road. We can stock up on snacks for the trip."

Huey eyed him skeptically. "How are we even getting there? No job, no money…"

"I got you," Doug said confidently. "Trust me, I wouldn't steer you wrong."

Huey scratched his head, remembering past times when Doug had said the same thing—times that didn't end well.
"Alright," he muttered, "but if this goes south, I'm not taking the blame. You know what happened last time. Mom nearly killed us!"

Doug smirked. "Don't worry, little bro. I've got a plan."

With backpacks slung and a grocery bag full of snacks from their mom's kitchen, the brothers caught a Greyhound bus from Texas to Durham, North Carolina.

After a long ride, they stepped off the bus and inhaled the cool country air.

"Smell that?" Doug said, stretching. "That's freedom."

"It's also cold," Huey replied, rubbing his arms. "This isn't Texas weather. Did you at least call Aunt Mable?"

Doug hesitated. "I meant to…"

Huey's eyes widened. "Doug!"

"I know, I know. But I'm telling you—they won't mind us dropping in. We family!"

Huey sighed. "You always say that."

They grabbed a taxi and made their way to Aunt Mable and Uncle LeRoy's home. As the car pulled up, both boys stared out the window in awe.

"Man, look at this place," Doug said. "They living large!"

"Retirement must be good," Huey added.

Doug grinned. "You need a job before you start dreaming about retirement."

"And you don't?" Huey shot back.

They approached the door and rang the bell. After a moment, Uncle LeRoy answered, a look of surprise etched across his face.

"Who is it?"

"It's Doug and Huey," Doug called out. "We came to visit!"

Uncle LeRoy raised an eyebrow. "Doug and Huey? From Texas? Unannounced?"

He opened the door, still processing the sight of the two grown boys standing on his porch.

"What brings you all this way?" Thousands of miles across country. Do tell.

"We were in the neighborhood," Doug replied sheepishly.

Huey gave a small wave. "Hey, Uncle LeRoy. Is Aunt Mable home?"

"She's at the store. Come on in. What's in the bags? You planning to stay a while?"

Doug shrugged. "Maybe a day or two. Or three…"

"Uh-huh," Uncle LeRoy said, stepping aside.

As the boys dropped their bags and made their way to the kitchen, Uncle LeRoy picked up the phone and dialed Aunt Mable.

"They just showed up," he said, shaking his head. "Yep. Becky's boys. No heads up."

Doug and Huey, meanwhile, were raiding the refrigerator. Sandwiches turned into a full meal. Plates piled high. The kitchen looked like Thanksgiving.

When Uncle LeRoy walked in, his eyes widened. "I thought you were making a sandwich. Not preparing a feast."

Doug grinned. "You said to make ourselves at home."

Huey nodded; mouth full. "That's what you said!"

Later, Doug looked out at the sliding glass door. "Huey, look, look, look at that! They have a hot tub bro!"

Huey dropped his sandwich. "For real?"

"Yep," Doug said. "We about to live large."

"Shouldn't we ask?"

Doug shrugged. "He already said make ourselves at home."

The brothers changed into swim trunks and slid into the steaming hot tub like kings.

"This is the life," Huey sighed.

"It sure is," Doug agreed.

They joked, splashed, and leaned back, gazing at the stars.

"Maybe this isn't just a weekend trip," Huey said.

Doug nodded. "Maybe it's the start of something new."

Chapter Two

SETTLING IN

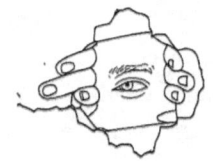

As the evening progresses, Aunt Mable finishes her call with Becky, reassuring her sister that the boys are safe and sound. Becky, although still upset, is relieved to know they're with family. Meanwhile, Doug and Huey, having finished their conversation with their mother, decide to make the most of their time at Aunt Mable and Uncle LeRoy's home.

The next day, Aunt Mable sits down with Doug and Huey to have a heart-to-heart conversation. She talks to them about the importance of taking responsibility for their actions and making positive choices for their future. She encourages them to consider their options carefully and to not be afraid to ask for help when they need it.

Uncle LeRoy takes the boys under his wing and teaches them some valuable life skills, such as basic car maintenance and household repairs. He shares stories from his own experiences and offers guidance on how to navigate the challenges of adulthood.

As the days pass, Doug and Huey gradually settle into a routine at Aunt Mable and Uncle LeRoy's home. They help out around the house, run errands, and even start looking for job opportunities in the area. With the love and support of their extended family, they begin to feel more confident about their future prospects.

Eventually, Becky comes to visit, and after some initial tension, she and the boys are able to reconcile. She admits that she was worried sick about them and apologizes for overreacting. Doug and Huey promise to communicate better in the future and to keep her informed about their plans.

Chapter Three

NEW RULES, NEW RHYTHMS

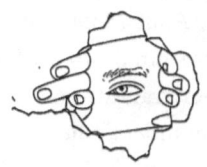

Doug woke up to the smell of sizzling bacon and the faint sound of gospel music playing from the kitchen radio. It was a peaceful contrast to the chaos back home. He stretched out on the soft guest mattress, feeling more rested than he had in weeks. Huey, still half-asleep, groaned from the other side of the room.

"Man, what time is it?" he mumbled.

Doug peeked at the clock. "Seven-thirty. Aunt Mable must be on one this morning."

By the time they made it to the kitchen, Aunt Mable was already plating up breakfast. "Good morning, boys! Breakfast is ready. And after you eat, we're doing a little cleanup. No freeloaders in this house," she added with a teasing wink.

They ate quickly, then got their marching orders: clean the guest room, sweep the porch, organize the garage.

Uncle LeRoy chimed in with, "And I'm showing you two how to check oil levels and change a tire later. Can't have y'all out here clueless."

Despite the grumbling, the boys took it in stride. Doug nearly knocked over a can of paint while sorting the garage shelves, and Huey got chased by a wasp while sweeping. The work was hard, but there were plenty of laughs too.

Later that afternoon, Aunt Mable introduced them to Sister Gladys, her chatty neighbor from down the block, who immediately tried to set Huey up with her granddaughter.

"That boy got good shoulders," she whispered loud enough for everyone to hear. Doug nearly choked on his lemonade.

In the evenings, Uncle LeRoy sat them down to watch old sports documentaries or walk them through DIY home repair tutorials. He kept it real, sharing the mistakes he made as a young man and how he turned things around. Both boys soaked it in.

By the end of the week, Doug and Huey had developed a rhythm. They weren't just houseguests anymore — they were contributing. It felt good. Real good.

But just as things began to settle, a new challenge arrived: the local community center was hiring for part-time help — and Aunt Mable was already filling out applications for them.

"Time to see what you're really made of," she said, sliding the papers across the table.

Doug and Huey exchanged a nervous look.

Their journey was only beginning.

Chapter Four

THE JOB HUNT

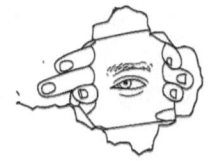

Doug sat on the edge of the guest bed, staring at the application in his hand.

"Man, I don't even know what to put under 'work experience,'" he muttered.

Huey, sitting cross-legged on the floor, was already scribbling down answers.

"Just write the truth, man. We helped Mom around the house, volunteered at the church food pantry a few times... that counts for something, right?"

Doug groaned. "This feels like a setup."

"It's a chance," Huey replied. "We came all the way out here. Might as well try."

The next morning, Aunt Mable handed them a pair of ironed button-down shirts and encouraged them to look presentable.

"You're walking into someone's business. First impressions count."

Their first stop was the community center. Doug tried to sound confident during the short interview, but when asked about conflict resolution, he froze. Huey stepped in to talk about helping mediate arguments between cousins during summer camp. The center director smiled, clearly amused, and told them she'd be in touch.

They stopped at two more places — a grocery store and a local hardware shop. At the hardware store, Huey impressed the owner by correctly naming tools on the wall, thanks to Uncle LeRoy's crash course.

The next few days were filled with nerves and hopeful waiting. On Friday morning, a call came in.

"Hello, may I speak with Huey? This is Miss Johnson from the community center. We'd like to offer you a part-time position working with our after-school program."

Huey's face lit up. Doug offered a proud high-five.

"What about me?" Doug asked jokingly.

Miss Johnson chuckled. "Still reviewing applications. But tell Doug to check in at the front desk on Monday. We may have something for him, too."

That evening, the family celebrated with Aunt Mable's famous baked chicken and sweet tea. Uncle LeRoy slapped both boys on the back.

"Now you're earning your keep. Feels good, don't it?"

Doug nodded. For once, it really did.

Chapter Five

NEW FACES, NEW CHALLENGES

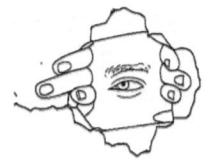

By Monday morning, Doug had a new job — helping the maintenance team at the community center. It wasn't glamorous, but it was honest work, and for the first time, he was earning his own money.

The center buzzed with activity. Kids played basketball, teens worked on computers, and volunteers ran programs in every corner. That's where Doug and Huey met Alonzo — a soft-spoken, no-nonsense youth mentor who quickly became a guiding voice.

"You two got good hearts," Alonzo said, watching Doug sweep the gym floor. "But you need structure. We all do. Stick with this place long enough, and you might find out what you're made of."

Huey was assigned to help Ms. Denise, a fiery, retired English teacher who ran the after-school homework club. She didn't tolerate laziness, and Huey learned fast that she expected the best from everyone — including him.

Meanwhile, Doug started clashing with Marcus, one of the other young maintenance workers. Marcus, a local with a chip on his shoulder, saw Doug as an outsider. Their tension simmered during every shift.

—

One afternoon, Marcus cornered Doug behind the rec hall. "Y'all just passing through, huh? Think you better than the rest of us?"

Doug bristled. "I'm just here to work, man. Not trying to be better than anyone."

"Then act like it," Marcus snapped, shoving past him.

The tension didn't go unnoticed. Alonzo pulled Doug aside later that week.

"People carry stuff, Doug. Pain, pride, fear. If you want to be a man, learn to listen before you fight."

Doug nodded slowly, realizing this was about more than just a job.

At home, Aunt Mable and Uncle LeRoy continued to cheer the boys on, but they also started pushing harder. Curfews were enforced. Chores doubled. Expectations rose.

—

One night at dinner, Aunt Mable turned to them both. "What's your five-year plan?"

Doug blinked. "Five years? I'm still trying to figure out tomorrow."

Huey laughed, but Aunt Mable wasn't joking.

"You've got potential, boys. But potential means nothing without a plan. Think about that."

As fall settled in, change filled the air. Doug and Huey weren't just growing — they were becoming. And life in Durham, with its small-town quirks and tough love lessons, was shaping them more than they expected.

Chapter Six

TURNING POINTS

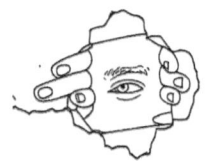

It started with a phone call late one Thursday night. Doug had forgotten to lock up a supply closet at the community center, and a group of kids got into it after hours. Nothing was stolen, but the center director wasn't happy.

"Careless mistakes can lead to real consequences," she said the next morning. "You've got to be more responsible."

Doug apologized, but the weight of it hit hard. He'd finally been doing something right, and now it felt like he was slipping again.

That night, Doug sat on the back porch, head down. Huey joined him with two cans of soda.

"You alright?" Huey asked.

"I messed up. And it's like... one mistake and everyone looks at you different."

"Doug," Huey said, "you're not the same guy who left Texas. You owned up to it. That matters."

Doug glanced at him, then nodded. "Thanks, bro."

The next day, Miss Denise had a moment of her own with Huey. One of the kids in the homework club had called him out: "You ain't a real teacher. You don't even talk like one."

Huey was stunned. He told Miss Denise he didn't belong.

She fixed on him with a sharp glare. "Every adult I know started out feeling like they didn't belong. That's not a reason to stop. It's the reason to keep going."

Her words stuck.

—

The weekend brought another surprise — Becky showed up unannounced.

She pulled into the driveway with her usual energy and a bag of groceries in her arms. "Figured I'd return the favor," she joked.

At first, dinner was awkward. Becky questioned the chores, the job hours, and the neighborhood.

But later that night, Huey caught her smiling as she watched him help Aunt Mable dry dishes.

"I see it now," Becky said softly to Mable. "They're really trying."

"They are," Mable replied. "And they're getting there."

The next morning, before Becky left, she pulled Doug into a hug.

"I'm proud of you," she whispered.

Doug was speechless.

As the leaves turned and the air chilled, life settled into something steady. Marcus even began warming up to Doug — cracking jokes during lunch breaks and nodding hello.

—

One afternoon, Alonzo asked Doug to help mentor one of the newer kids in the gym.

"Me?" Doug asked.

"You," Alonzo said. "Time to pay it forward."

Doug accepted, and for the first time, he didn't feel like a visitor. He felt like he belonged.

Chapter Seven

A NEW FOUNDATION

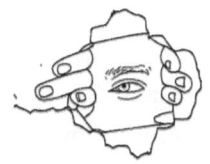

The next big shift came on a Sunday morning.

Aunt Mable, dressed in a plum-colored hat and matching heels, stood by the front door. "Time to go to church, boys."

Doug looked up from the couch. "Church?"

"Yep," Uncle LeRoy added, adjusting his tie. "There's more to life than work and chores. You need spiritual grounding too."

Reluctantly, Doug and Huey got dressed. Neither had been in a church service in years, but they followed their aunt and uncle into the small brick building tucked on the corner of Elm Street.

The warmth inside surprised them. Members greeted them with handshakes and hugs, and the choir's opening hymn stirred something they hadn't felt in a long time.

After service, they stayed for a youth lunch. That's where they met Pastor Jay — a down-to-earth, jeans-and-boots type with a laugh that filled the room.

"I hear y'all are new to Durham," he said, nodding. "Let me know if you ever want to talk or get involved."

Huey looked at Doug. For the first time in a while, they both nodded.

—

Over the next few weeks, the church became a second home. Huey joined a mentoring program for boys. Doug helped organize community cleanup events with the men's ministry. Their calendar filled up fast, but so did their hearts.

It wasn't always easy. Doug still struggled with focus. Huey still doubted himself. But the church gave them direction and surrounded them with people who genuinely cared.

As they began attending weekly Bible study, both brothers found themselves leaning into the scriptures. One Wednesday evening, Pastor Jay taught from Proverbs 3:5–6: "Trust in the Lord with all your heart and lean not on your own understanding; in all your ways submit to him, and he will make your paths straight."

Those words hit home.

Afterward, Doug whispered to Huey, "I think that's what we've been missing all along. Trust. Not in ourselves, but in something bigger."

Huey nodded slowly. "Yeah, maybe it's time we stop trying to figure it all out on our own."

—

The following Sunday, both boys walked to the altar, not because someone told them to, but because something inside them shifted. They prayed. They cried. And they surrendered.

That moment marked a new chapter — not just in Durham, but in their hearts. It wasn't about being perfect. It was about letting go of control and letting God direct their paths.

—

At dinner one night, Aunt Mable beamed. "You boys have found your stride."

Uncle LeRoy raised a glass of sweet tea. "To new beginnings."

They clinked glasses. Doug leaned back, smiling. He hadn't imagined any of this when they boarded that Greyhound bus. But somehow, in the most unexpected place, they were building a new foundation.

And it felt like home.

Chapter Eight

RISING TO THE CALL

With the boys now rooted in their spiritual journey and daily life in Durham, a new chapter of responsibility began. At the community center, Miss Johnson pulled Huey aside after a particularly lively youth mentoring session.

"Huey, you ever thought about leading your own workshop?" she asked.

Huey blinked. "Me? Lead?"

"Yes, you. The kids respond to you. You've got something to say, and they're listening."

That evening, Huey brought it up to Doug. "Man, what if I mess up? What if I can't do it?"

Doug grinned. "Then you mess up. But you keep showing up. Just like we've been doing."

Meanwhile, Doug was offered a bigger role helping Alonzo supervise the community gym. With Marcus now more of a friend than a rival, the two had begun working as a team. The space had become something more than just a job—it was a mission.

—

Back at church, Pastor Jay introduced a new youth-led worship night. He approached the brothers to help coordinate it.

"I'm trusting you two," he said. "This is your generation. Use your voice."

They hesitated—but not for long.

Doug handled the setup and music coordination while Huey, after much prayer and a few nerves, prepared a short talk. The night arrived, and the sanctuary was full of young faces—curious, skeptical, hopeful.

Huey stepped up, heart pounding. He shared a piece of their story: growing up in chaos, making mistakes, and learning to trust God.

"You don't have to be perfect to be used," he said. "You just have to be willing."

The room was silent for a beat. Then came claps. Nods. And quiet tears.

Afterward, Pastor Jay slapped a hand on Doug's shoulder. "You boys are doing something real. Keep pressing forward."

—

At home, Aunt Mable couldn't stop smiling. Uncle LeRoy offered extra dessert that night—a rare gesture.

Later, Doug and Huey sat in the quiet backyard, the stars overhead as vivid as that first hot tub night.

"Feels like we've been given a purpose," Doug said.

"Not given," Huey replied. "Revealed. We just needed to be still long enough to hear it."

They sat in the peace of that revelation—brothers, believers, and builders of something far greater than either of us had imagined when the journey began.

Chapter Nine

HEALTH WAKE-UP CALL

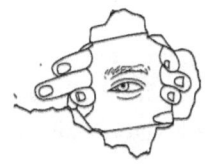

It started with Huey feeling lightheaded after an intense youth program at the community center. He brushed it off at first, but Aunt Mable insisted he see a doctor. Doug tagged along, more out of support than concern until the doctor pulled out the blood pressure cuff.

"Your blood pressure is dangerously high," Dr. Lambert said, looking directly at Huey. "You're young, but this isn't something you can ignore."

Doug tried to lighten the mood. "He eats too many biscuits. That's the problem."

Dr. Lambert didn't laugh. She turned to Doug. "And you—when was the last time your knees didn't ache?"

Doug blinked. "Uh… been a while."

"Let's take a look." Minutes later, she confirmed what Doug had been ignoring: early signs of joint strain from excess weight.

"You both need to take this seriously," she said. "Weight-related issues are creeping up. If you don't make changes now, you'll be dealing with more than discomfort—think diabetes, heart disease, limited mobility."

On the ride home, the mood was quiet. No jokes. Just reflection.

That night, they brought it up at dinner. Aunt Mable set down her fork.

"Health is wealth, boys. We want you around for the long haul."

Uncle LeRoy added, "We'll make changes with you. No more sweet tea every night. More veggies. Walks after dinner."

True to their word, the whole household joined in. Doug and Huey started walking the neighborhood trail with Uncle LeRoy. Huey tried a dance fitness class with Sister Gladys—who moved better than most twenty-year-olds.

Meals became cleaner. Groceries changed. The work was hard—but their bodies slowly responded.

—

One morning, Doug stood in the mirror. "Hey, I can see my chin again."

Huey laughed. "Just one of them?"

They kept at it—not for appearances, but for life.

Because for the first time, they truly understood: if they wanted to fulfill their purpose, they had to be around long enough to live it.

Chapter Ten

MAMA KNOWS BEST

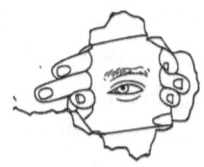

A few days after their doctor's visit, the boys were finishing a walk around the neighborhood trail when Doug's phone rang. He glanced at the screen.

"Uh oh," he said. "It's Mom."

Huey groaned. "You think she knows?"

Doug tapped answer. "Hey, Ma."

Becky's voice came through loud and clear. "Hey baby. Just checking on you two. You been quiet lately. Everything alright?"

Doug hesitated. "Yeah… yeah, we're good."

Huey leaned closer. "Tell her."

Doug sighed and put the phone on speaker.

"Actually, Ma… we went to the doctor. Huey wasn't feeling well."

Becky's tone sharpened. "What happened?"

Huey jumped in. "I'm okay now, but they said I had high blood pressure. Doug's knees have been acting up too."

There was a pause on the other end.

"High blood pressure? Lord, you boys have to take better care of yourselves! And Doug, your knees?"

"I'm working on it, Ma. We both are," Doug said quickly.

Huey added, "We're eating better. Walking every day. Even Aunt Mable's cutting back on the sweet tea."

Becky's voice softened. "That makes me feel better. I worry, y'all know that. But I'm proud of you. That's real grown-up stuff—facing things instead of hiding from them."

Doug and Huey looked at each other, smiles forming.

"We just realized if we want to keep doing all this good stuff—church, community center, everything—we need to be healthy enough to do it," Doug said.

"Well, amen to that," Becky said. "And just know, I'm still your mama. You ever feel off, I better be the first one to know, you hear me?"

"Yes ma'am," both brothers said in unison.

As they ended the call, Huey pocketed the phone. "She took that better than I thought."

Doug laughed. "I think we're finally giving her something to brag about."

—

The next day, a package arrived from Becky—a care box packed with herbal teas, vitamins, and two pairs of matching walking shoes.

Doug held up the note inside and read aloud: "To my healthy boys. Keep walking. Keep praying. Love, Mom."

They smiled, knowing they weren't just walking a trail—they were walking into their future. And now, they had all the support they needed, every step of the way.

Chapter Eleven

A PATH FORWARD

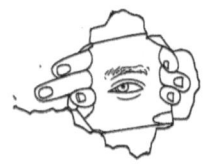

The chill of early winter had begun to settle over Durham. Scarves, coats, and warm tea became part of the boys' new daily rhythm. One evening, as they wrapped up dinner and rinsed dishes, Aunt Mable cleared her throat and motioned for them to sit.

"I've been thinking," she said, drying her hands on a dish towel. "You boys are doing well—working, eating right, keeping the faith. But what's next?"

Doug and Huey glanced at each other.

"I mean long-term," she continued. "You ever thought about taking a class or learning a trade?"

Uncle LeRoy joined in, sitting down across from them. "College ain't the only path—but education of some kind is key. I learned a trade at your age. It carried me a long way."

Huey scratched his head. "We've talked about it... kinda. But it's hard to know what direction to take."

"That's why you pray on it," Aunt Mable said, matter-of-factly. "Ask God to show you where your gifts can be used."

That night, Doug and Huey sat in their room with a laptop and a notebook. They began jotting down ideas: computer repair, culinary arts, HVAC certification, early childhood education, graphic design.

Doug looked at Huey. "Man, I didn't even know half this stuff was an option."

"Right?" Huey said. "I kinda want to learn how to fix cars. Like for real."

Doug grinned. "I've been thinking about music production. Maybe even teaching it. With what we've been doing at the community center... it just feels right."

—

Later that week, Aunt Mable drove them to the local community college. A guidance counselor walked them through programs, financial aid, and flexible schedules. For the first time in a long while, the future didn't feel distant. It felt possible.

That evening, they knelt beside their beds and prayed.

"God," Doug said softly, "we want to keep walking with You. Just help us know where to put our next step."

Huey echoed, "We're listening now. Just lead the way."

And for the first time, their path forward felt more than hopeful—it felt anointed.

Chapter Twelve

COMMITMENT AND COURSEWORK

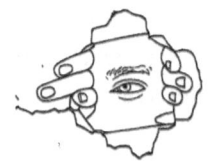

Doug and Huey stared at their course catalogs like explorers facing uncharted territory. Classes in auto tech, audio engineering, business basics, and graphic design stared back at them. They'd narrowed it down—Huey signed up for an introductory auto repair class and Doug for a digital music production workshop.

The first day was nerve-wracking.

Huey walked into his shop class full of grease-stained overalls and buzzing tools. He felt out of place. "Man, I don't know nothin' about spark plugs," he whispered to himself.

But by the end of the week, he could name engine components and diagnose basic problems. His instructor, Mr. Simmons, gave him a nod. "You've got hands-on talent, Huey. Keep showing up."

Meanwhile, Doug sat in a soundproofed lab, mesmerized by beat machines and mixing software. The instructor gave them a project—remix a song using live-recorded samples. Doug stayed after class, playing with tracks until he heard something he liked. For the first time in his life, school didn't feel like a chore.

—

Back home, Aunt Mable had them studying at the dining table every night. Uncle LeRoy quizzed them from the couch.

"Transmission or alternator?"

"Alternator!" Huey shouted.

"EQ or reverb?"

"Reverb!" Doug answered, grinning.

Still, balancing it all wasn't easy. Doug nearly missed a homework deadline after pulling double duty at the community center. Huey overslept and was late to class twice in one week.

"I can't do this," Doug muttered one night, slumped over his laptop.

Aunt Mable sat beside him. "Yes, you can. Progress isn't always a straight line. Sometimes it zigs and zags, but you keep walking it."

Doug smiled weakly. "You're like Yoda with a Southern drawl."

They both laughed.

Later that night, the boys sat in their room, Bibles open between them. They prayed for endurance, wisdom, and peace.

Huey looked up. "This ain't just about jobs. It's about building something bigger, right?"

Doug nodded. "Our lives. Our future. Our purpose."

They weren't just taking classes. They were laying bricks—one skill, one choice, one prayer at a time—for the life they were finally ready to live.

Chapter Thirteen

NEW FRIENDSHIPS, NEW TEMPTATIONS

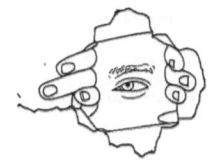

The spring semester brought new faces, new energy, and new challenges. On campus, Doug met Jaylen, a fellow music production student with quick wit and endless connections. They clicked immediately.

"You ever come to 'The Loop'?" Jaylen asked one afternoon.

Doug shook his head.

"It's a student open-mic spot on Thursdays. All the up-and-comers hang there. I think you'd vibe."

Doug hesitated, thinking of his evening study schedule—and Pastor Jay's Thursday Bible group—but curiosity got the better of him.

Huey, meanwhile, had made friends in his auto tech class, especially with a guy named Rico. Rico was smooth-talking, always had a story, and seemed to have life figured out.

"Man, you stress too much," Rico told Huey one day. "Skip class Friday, hit the track with us. You need to loosen up."

Temptation knocked. Doug visited The Loop, and it was electric. DJs spinning, students rapping, lights low and bass high. He felt alive—and conflicted.

Huey skipped a class to hang with Rico and his friends. What started as a harmless outing led to a wild night—and a minor car accident that left Huey shaken but unharmed.

That night, he stood in Aunt Mable's kitchen, eyes lowered. "I messed up. Bad."

She hugged him. "You didn't mess up. You got a wake-up call. Now what are you going to do with it?"

Doug didn't feel much better. He had stayed out too late and missed his morning devotional with Pastor Jay.

"I thought I was just being social," he confessed to Alonzo. "But it's easy to lose track out there."

Alonzo nodded. "The world will always offer noise. You've got to choose your soundtrack."

—

That Sunday, both brothers went to the altar. Again. Not because they had fallen all the way off, but because they needed a reset.

Pastor Jay prayed over them. "Lord, help these young men see that temptation isn't failure. It's a moment—a test. And they're still on the path You designed."

—

The week after, Doug politely declined Jaylen's invite. Huey returned to class with a renewed focus.

Mistakes didn't define them—but their choices moving forward would.

The foundation was still there.

And they were still building.

Chapter Fourteen

WHEN LIFE HITS HOME

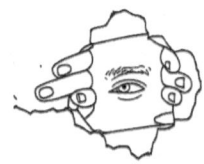

It started like any other Sunday. Aunt Mable was in the kitchen prepping a roast. Uncle LeRoy was in the garage tinkering with an old lawnmower. Doug and Huey were getting ready for church when a loud thump echoed through the house.

They rushed to the garage to find Uncle LeRoy on one knee, gripping his chest.

"LeRoy!" Aunt Mable screamed from the back door.

Huey helped him sit down while Doug grabbed the phone. Minutes later, the paramedics arrived.

Thankfully, it wasn't a heart attack—but it was a wake-up call. Uncle LeRoy had ignored his blood pressure and had been overexerting himself.

At the hospital, he looked at the boys. "Y'all be smarter than me. Don't ignore the warning signs."

Back home, the house felt quieter. Slower. Aunt Mable kept her usual strength, but they could tell she was worried. Doug and Huey stepped up—shopping, cleaning, managing the yard.

—

Late one evening, after putting up groceries, Huey said, "Man, I thought he was invincible."

Doug nodded. "Yeah. Seeing him like that shook me."

The next morning, they sat with Aunt Mable at the table, flipping through a Bible study guide.

"I think we need to do more than just react to life," Huey said. "We need to live on purpose. Like Unc always says."

Doug added, "We should put together a health day at the community center. Bring in nurses, offer screenings—get people talking about this stuff."

Aunt Mable smiled. "Now that's purpose."

They brought the idea to Pastor Jay and Miss Johnson, and the planning began. Flyers went out, volunteers signed up, and local nurses offered their time.

The health day was a success. Over sixty people came through. Doug DJ'd. Huey managed the flow of activities. Uncle LeRoy, now recovering well, gave a heartfelt talk about taking care of yourself before it's too late.

Later that night, he pulled the boys aside.

"You two did good. Real good. Makes an old man proud."

Doug smiled. "You're not old, Unc. Just classic."

They all laughed.

That night, Doug and Huey sat outside beneath the stars.

"Crazy how fast things can change," Huey said.

Doug nodded. "Yeah. But maybe that's why we've got to stay ready. Stay grounded. We've got too much to live for now."

And they knew in their hearts—this wasn't just about overcoming setbacks anymore. It was about becoming the men they were meant to be.

Chapter Fifteen

STEPPING INTO LEGACY

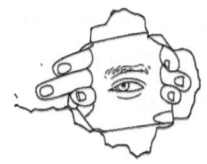

The week after the health day, something shifted. Pastor Jay pulled Doug aside after Sunday service.

"You ever think about doing this full-time?" he asked.

"Church stuff?" Doug raised a brow.

"Ministry. Mentorship. Music. Whatever God has placed in your heart."

Doug didn't know how to answer. He'd been toying with an idea—what if he built a small recording space at the community center to teach music production? He'd even started pricing equipment online.

Later that night, Doug shared the thought with Alonzo. "You think I'm biting off too much?"

Alonzo grinned. "I think you're answering the call."

Meanwhile, Huey was coming into his own. Ms. Denise had nominated him to lead a weekend workshop for young men called Fix-It and Figure-It-Out. It blended basic auto maintenance with talks about manhood, faith, and discipline.

Huey was nervous, but the first session drew a full crowd—and afterward, one of the boys said, "You make stuff make sense."

That stuck with him.

At home, Aunt Mable noticed the shift.

"You two ain't boys anymore," she said one evening as they cleared dishes. "You're becoming builders. Of lives. Of legacy."

Doug laughed. "Legacy? I'm just trying to get these church kids to stay on beat."

But deep down, he felt it too.

—

The following week, Doug met someone. Her name was Ayana— bright smile, youth ministry volunteer, and unapologetically honest.

"I see what you're doing," she told Doug after youth worship night. "It matters."

They started talking more. Sharing scripture. Trading playlists. It was early, but real.

Huey noticed—and teased him relentlessly.

"Looks like big bro finally got some competition for the mirror."

"I got depth, man," Doug replied, chuckling.

Huey wasn't far behind. He reconnected with a classmate, Selena, who invited him to volunteer at a weekend food drive. They bonded over cars, faith, and favorite soul food spots.

Amid these new relationships, Becky called with unexpected news. "Boys, I'm thinking about taking a job out of state."

"You moving?" Huey asked, surprised.

"Possibly. But I need to know—are you two okay? Like really okay?"

There was a pause.

"We're more than okay," Doug said. "We're growing. We're grounded. And Mom... we're proud of who we're becoming."

Becky sniffled. "I needed to hear that. I really did."

—

The next Sunday, Pastor Jay called them to the front of the church.

"These two young men didn't just find their way—they're helping others find theirs. Let's thank God for their obedience and their journey."

Applause filled the sanctuary.

Doug and Huey stood side by side, humbled and emotional.

And in that moment, they knew: this wasn't just a story of two brothers who left home.

It was the beginning of something bigger—a legacy just getting started.

Chapter Sixteen

TOUGH DECISIONS

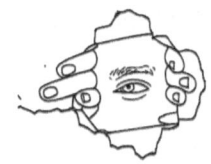

The recognition at church lit a fire under Doug and Huey. With their confidence growing, new opportunities started rolling in—and so did difficult choices.

Huey was the first to face one.

Mr. Simmons, his auto tech instructor, pulled him aside after class. "There's a shop downtown looking for an apprentice. Paid, full-time. They need someone reliable, and I gave them your name."

Huey was flattered—but the job meant cutting back on his classes.

That night at dinner, he brought it up.

"I don't want to quit school," he said. "But this could help me get a foot in the door."

Uncle LeRoy leaned back in his chair. "Sometimes opportunities come before the degree. If you stay focused, you can make both work."

Doug, meanwhile, received an email from a local nonprofit music program in Atlanta. They'd seen a clip of his youth worship session online and invited him to apply for a six-month internship. Housing and stipend included.

He brought the letter to Pastor Jay.

"I don't want to leave everything we've built here," Doug admitted.

Pastor Jay smiled. "Son, nothing you've built here disappears. If God is opening a door, don't let fear keep you in the hallway."

For days, the brothers prayed, talked, and paced the backyard.

"If we both do this, we're splitting up," Huey said.

"Not splitting up," Doug replied. "Just growing in different directions."

Eventually, they made their decisions. Huey accepted the apprenticeship but promised to continue his certification classes part-time. Doug submitted his application to the internship—and was accepted within a week.

—

The night before Doug left for Atlanta, they sat on the porch, a little quieter than usual.

"You scared?" Huey asked.

"Terrified," Doug said. "But I'm excited too."

Huey nodded. "I'm proud of you, man. For real."

Doug reached out his fist. "We said we'd do this together. Just didn't say we'd do it all in the same zip code."

Huey bumped his fist with a grin. "We still are. Just walking separate paths—with the same mission."

And with that, the next chapter of their journey began—not side by side, but always connected, heart to heart, purpose to purpose.

Chapter Seventeen

A SEASON APART

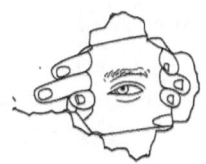

The morning Doug left for Atlanta, the house was unusually quiet. Aunt Mable hugged him three times before he even stepped out the door.

"Don't forget to call. And don't be so busy building your future that you forget your present," she said, dabbing her eyes.

Uncle LeRoy nodded solemnly. "Take care of yourself. Make good choices. And represent this family right."

Huey stood by the front porch, hands in his hoodie pockets. "Call me when you land, alright?"

Doug gave him a long hug. "I will. Hold it down for us."

As the car pulled away, the porch felt emptier than usual.

Back in Durham, Huey jumped into his apprenticeship.

The garage was gritty and hot, but he loved the rhythm. He found himself mentoring a younger teen named Xavier—quick-tempered but talented.

"You remind me of myself," Huey told him one day. "Headstrong, but worth the work."

—

Meanwhile in Atlanta, Doug was immersed in the world of soundboards, youth mentorship, and late-night studio sessions. He kept a photo of the Durham church team taped inside his notebook.

He called home often—sometimes for advice, other times just to hear familiar voices. He and Huey talked nearly every other night.

"You eating right?" Huey asked during one call.

"I had a kale salad last week."

"Kale salad? Who are you and what did you do with my brother?"

They laughed. But sometimes the calls were deeper.

"I miss y'all," Doug admitted. "I didn't realize how much Durham grounded me."

"You're doing what you're called to do," Huey said. "And I'm proud of you."

The months passed. Seasons changed. And growth continued.

Huey finished his auto tech certification. Doug led a citywide youth music showcase.

—

When Doug finally returned to Durham for a weekend visit, Aunt Mable cooked enough for a small army. Uncle LeRoy let him sleep in—just for one day.

That evening, Doug and Huey sat under the stars again.

"Still feels like home," Doug said.

"It always will," Huey replied.

And with the night breeze rustling through the trees, they sat in silence—grateful for the path behind them and ready for what lay ahead.

Chapter Eighteen

LETTERS AND LESSONS

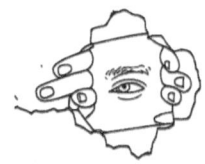

As Doug settled into life in Atlanta and Huey grew more confident in his role back home, the brothers found new ways to stay close—handwritten letters, voice notes, and long Sunday evening phone calls.

One evening, Huey sat at the kitchen table with a pen and notebook, deciding to write a letter instead of sending a text. "Dear Doug," he wrote, "You wouldn't believe how Xavier's doing. He actually fixed a carburetor today without help. I think he's finally believing in himself. Just like I'm starting to."

Across state lines, Doug read the letter out loud in his dorm room. Smiling, he pulled out his journal to respond.

"Dear Huey, You should've seen these kids last night. We hosted a beat battle, and one of the shyest girls in the program took

home first place. She told me she never felt heard until now. Man…
this is what it's about."

Each note shared stories, fears, wins, and lessons. Doug talked
about leading a Bible study with other interns and the challenge of
staying spiritually grounded amid city distractions. Huey reflected
on stepping up at the shop when his supervisor took medical leave.

Even their mentors chimed in—Pastor Jay sent Doug a
devotional, while Mr. Simmons wrote a recommendation letter for
Huey's promotion.

In one letter, Doug ended with a quote from Proverbs: "As iron
sharpens iron, so one person sharpens another." He added, "Thanks
for always sharpening me, bro."

Huey taped that line above his bed.

The physical distance didn't weaken their bond—it refined it.
And as they continued walking their paths, they were becoming not
just better men, but better brothers, mentors, and leaders.

Because sometimes the strongest connections aren't built side
by side—but word by word, prayer by prayer, mile by mile.

Chapter Nineteen

QUIET HOUSE, FULL HEARTS

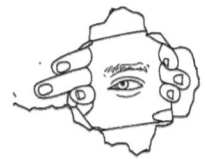

The mornings were quieter now. No sound of footsteps racing down the stairs, no music blaring from the guest room. Aunt Mable sipped her tea in the sunroom, staring out at the hydrangeas she and Huey had planted that spring. Uncle LeRoy, now retired from his garage tinkering, found himself staring at the tools Doug had once borrowed to fix a wobbly fence post.

"They kept the house lively," Mable said one morning, setting down her cup.

LeRoy nodded. "Too quiet without 'em."

The couple had grown used to the rhythm of young voices filling the home — laughter, questions, late-night fridge raids. Now, it was just the ticking clock and the hum of the refrigerator.

"I remember the day they showed up," Mable continued. "Didn't even call first. Just two big boys with overstuffed bags and a plan made out of thin air."

"And hungry," LeRoy chuckled. "I still ain't recovered from that first grocery bill."

They both laughed, but the air quickly turned thoughtful. Mable walked over to the mantle, tracing her fingers along a photo of the boys with their arms slung around her and LeRoy. Her eyes then drifted to another picture — their son, Pig, in his military uniform.

"I miss him too," she whispered.

LeRoy stood and joined her. "Me too. Every single day."

Pig had left home years ago, full of conviction and pride. His absence was deeply felt, especially now that Doug and Huey had gone too. Though their house was empty of sound, their hearts remained full.

"They reminded me of him," Mable said. "All that fire. All that potential. Just needed a little shaping."

"They've been shaped," LeRoy added. "And they're shaping others. That's what matters."

They sat together on the front porch that evening, side by side in silence. The sky turned golden, then navy blue.

As the streetlights buzzed on, Mable whispered, "I hope they know we're proud."

LeRoy squeezed her hand. "They know. And if they don't, we'll tell 'em again next time they call."

In the quiet, the memory of laughter echoed. And even in the stillness, love lived loudly.

Chapter Twenty

FULL CIRCLES

Doug and Huey returned to Durham under a soft spring sun, duffel bags in hand and stories etched across their faces. Aunt Mable met them at the door with teary eyes, arms wide. Uncle LeRoy stood a few steps behind, grinning like he'd just won the lottery.

"Now don't act like strangers," Mable said, pulling them in for hugs. "Get in here. I made sweet tea and peach cobbler."

Back in the kitchen, it felt like no time had passed. Doug shared his experiences in Atlanta—the music classes, the kids he mentored, the late-night studio sessions that turned into prayer meetings. Huey talked about Xavier's transformation, completing his own certification, and fixing his first car without help.

That night, they sat outside under familiar stars.

Huey said, "You know, we left with nothing but a bag of groceries and a prayer."

Doug nodded. "And came back with purpose."

—

The next week, Pastor Jay invited them to speak during Sunday service.

Huey stepped up first. "We didn't know what we were doing when we showed up in Durham. But this place, this family, this church... you gave us a chance."

Doug followed. "And now, we want to give that same chance to someone else."

The congregation erupted in applause.

—

Within a month, they launched The Foundation Project—a mentorship and skills-building initiative for young men in the community. Doug ran the creative lab: music production, storytelling, digital media. Huey handled the mechanics side: basic car repair, tool literacy, responsibility workshops.

They didn't do it alone. Alonzo joined as an advisor. Ms. Denise returned to teach financial literacy. Ayana and Selena helped coordinate outreach. Aunt Mable brought snacks to every meeting, and Uncle LeRoy taught Saturday workshops titled, "Fix It Like Your Life Depends On It."

It grew faster than they imagined.

—

One day, while packing up after a session, Doug looked at Huey. "Think Mom would believe this if she saw us now?"

Huey chuckled. "She'd probably ask who kidnapped her sons and replaced them with these responsible adults."

They laughed.

The book wasn't over. Life would still throw surprises, setbacks, and new chapters. But this story—the one that started with an unplanned trip and two boys looking for something more—had come full circle.

And it was just the beginning.

Chapter Twenty-One

THE REUNION

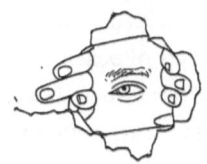

It was a warm summer Saturday when the doorbell rang at Aunt Mable's house. She wasn't expecting anyone, and Uncle LeRoy was in the backyard trimming the hedges. When she opened the door, her mouth dropped open.

"Well, don't just stand there looking surprised," Becky said with a wide smile. "You gonna let me in, or what?"

Behind her stood two cousins, her older sister Regina, and a niece Doug and Huey hadn't seen in years. Everyone carried bags of food, folding chairs, and boxed fans. Becky waved a small envelope in the air. "Thought y'all could use a surprise family reunion."

Aunt Mable's eyes filled with tears. "Girl, get in here. What are you doing?"

"We're celebrating," Becky said. "Doug and Huey. Their growth. Their foundation. And our family."

Word spread fast. By afternoon, the backyard was full of laughter, lawn games, and folding tables covered in covered dishes. Someone pulled out a Bluetooth speaker and started a line dance.

Huey grilled chicken while cracking jokes. Doug DJ'd from his laptop with a playlist called "From Texas to Purpose." Uncle LeRoy wore a new apron that read "Pitmaster in Chief," while Aunt Mable ran the drink station like a general.

When the music slowed and folks gathered in lawn chairs, Becky stood up, holding a plate of peach cobbler.

"I gave my boys a hard time when they left Texas. Thought they were running from something. Turns out, they were running toward who they were meant to be. And I couldn't be prouder."

Doug and Huey stood beside her, humbled. Doug cleared his throat.

"We couldn't have done it without all of you. This family, this town, this second chance… it changed everything."

Huey added, "And to any cousins out there still trying to figure life out — just know, there's always a way forward. And it usually starts with someone believing in you."

A round of applause followed. Laughter. Even a few tears.

As the sun dipped low and lightning bugs lit the yard, Aunt Mable leaned back in her chair.

"Look at this," she whispered to Uncle LeRoy. "This right here… this is legacy."

And for the first time in a long time, everything felt whole.

Chapter Twenty-Two

FROM BAGGAGE TO BELONGING

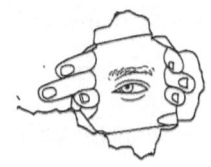

Weeks after the reunion, life in Durham found its steady rhythm again. The laughter from that day lingered in the walls of Aunt Mable's home. Every now and then, a leftover pan of cobbler or a forgotten folding chair reminded them of the joyful gathering that brought generations together.

One Friday afternoon, Huey was sweeping the community center when a teen named Khalil approached him. "Mr. Huey, you ever think about giving up?"

Huey looked up, smiling. "All the time. But family—blood or chosen—keeps me going."

That evening, Doug sat in the music room, guiding a student through sound mixing. He paused, watching the boy's face light up as a beat dropped just right. It reminded him of the day he first touched a soundboard and realized he had something worth sharing.

Later that night, back at the house, Doug and Huey sat with Aunt Mable and Uncle LeRoy under the soft porch light. The stars shimmered above them.

"You know," Doug said, "We showed up here with nothing. Not even a plan."

"But you had potential," Aunt Mable said. "And hearts open enough to let God and this family shape you."

Huey nodded. "We came as unexpected guests... but we stayed because of the bonds we built."

Uncle LeRoy leaned back in his chair. "Family ain't always planned. Sometimes it just shows up—and when it does, you feed it, guide it, and give it room to grow."

Doug looked at his brother. "Think we'll ever go back to Texas?"

Huey grinned. "Maybe for a visit. But our future? It's here."

They all sat quietly for a moment, breathing in the warm Carolina night.

The boys who once arrived unannounced with backpacks and uncertainty had become men—rooted in faith, driven by purpose, and bound by the love of the family that took them in.

Unexpected Guests: Family Bonds was never just a story of two brothers finding themselves. It was a testimony to what can happen when love opens the door, grace sets the table, and legacy invites you to stay.

And in that quiet moment beneath the stars, they knew the journey was far from over.

But they were ready—for whatever came next.

ACKNOWLEDGMENTS

This story would not be possible without the many hands, hearts, and prayers that shaped it.

To my husband, Thomas, and my incredible sons, William and TJ—thank you for walking this journey with me and always believing in what I could create. Your love is my anchor.

To my family and my Sands, Risky Business of Delta Sigma Theta Sorority, Inc. who loves me unconditionally, and to my MOTIV8 Church family whose prayers have lifted and carried me through every season—this story is also yours.

To the families who inspire me—thank you for showing what grace, patience, and love look like in real life. To my own Aunt Mables and Uncle LeRoys, your wisdom and generosity shine through every page.

To the young people on journeys of self-discovery: this book is for you. May you always find a porch light left on and a table with room for one more.

To my community, my mentors, and the youth I've had the honor of walking beside—thank you for your stories, your courage, and your faith.

And most of all, to GOD—thank You for turning unexpected moments into unforgettable testimonies.